GREAT SIEGE DAY

Saviour Pirotta

Photographs by Chris Fairclough

Hamish Hamilton   London

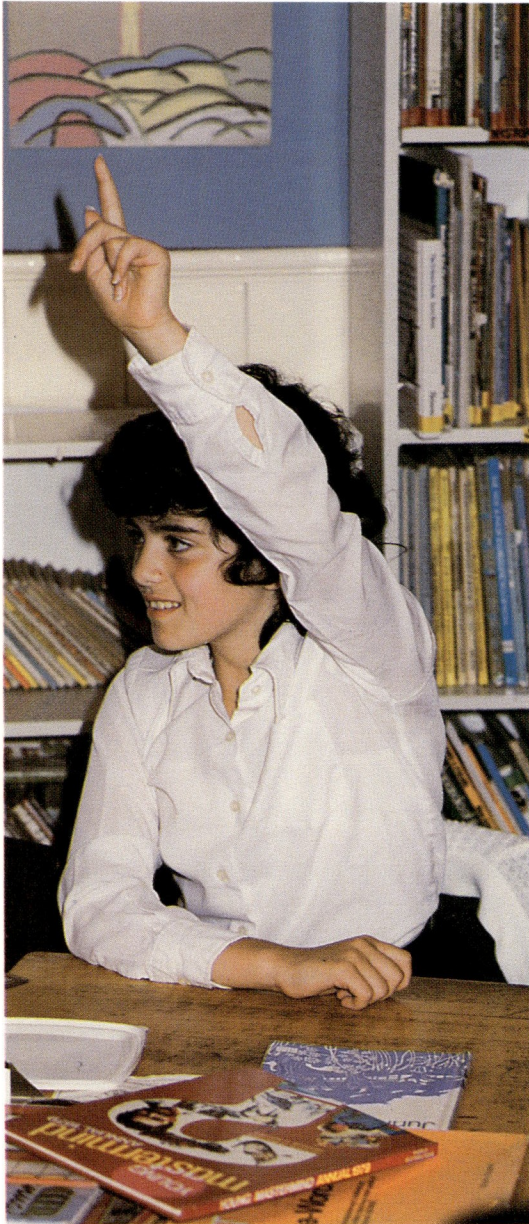

Today is the first day of school and the class is full of new faces. Miss Matthews asks the children to introduce themselves. Julie comes from Ghana. Gulianella is Italian. Peter was born in Ireland. And Fiona's parents come from Malta.

'Where is Malta?' some of the children ask. Miss Matthews shows them a map of the world. 'Malta is an island,' she says. 'Can anyone see it?'

Everyone looks very hard but no one can spot Malta. Only Fiona knows where it is. 'Here,' she says, pointing to a small dot between Italy and Africa. 'It's right in the middle of the Mediterranean Sea.'

'It's tiny,' Peter says. Miss Matthews agrees. 'Malta is so small,' she says, 'that a lot of people have had to go and live somewhere else. Many went to big countries like Canada and Australia where they could find work in big cities. But others preferred to settle somewhere nearer to home. They chose Britain.'

Everyone wants to know more about the Maltese so Fiona tells them all about Great Siege Day.

'In Malta,' Fiona explains, 'every village is dedicated to a patron saint. Each saint has his own birthday called a *festa*.

'The Maltese celebrate each one of these *festi* with lots of dancing and colourful pageants. They decorate the streets and eat a special sweet called *qubbajt*.'

Fiona has a photograph of what her granny's street looks like during a *festa*. She shows it to the class.

The biggest of the *festi* takes place on the 8th of September. Its proper name is Great Siege Day but the Maltese call it *Il-Vitorja* – Victory Day.

This is the birthday of God's mother – the Blessed Virgin Mary – and the date of a victory over Turkish pirates in 1565.

Fiona's father keeps a statue of a Maltese knight in the front hall to remind him of this special day.

Fiona and her family have a small *festa* with their friends at home.

The day before, Fiona helps to clean the house while Dad fills the fridge with beer and food. 'We must have lots to eat,' Dad says. 'In Malta people leave their doors open all throughout the *festa* so that people will know they are welcome to come inside and share the food.'

Fiona polishes the back door. Everything must be sparkling clean by Sunday.

'Where's Mummy?' Sabrina asks.
Dad thinks she's gone out to do some shopping.
'Come and help me prepare the altar,' he says.

Sabrina clears a shelf while Dad hangs a blue cloth with the Maltese
Cross on it. Then they put a small statue of the Virgin Mary in the
centre. Dad lights the candles.
'We must be very thankful to Mary,' Dad says. 'She has always
protected the Maltese people from trouble.'

Sabrina finds bits of candles all over the carpet. Dad has to clean them up. 'Feet off the floor!' he tells Sabrina.

After all the cleaning Fiona feels tired. 'Come on,' she says to Sabrina. 'Let's go and get some sweets.'
Sabrina hunts around for some *qubbajt*, the famous sweet which all Maltese children eat during the *festa*.

'We don't have any *qubbajt*,' Mrs Sethi and her daughter say. 'But maybe your family will send you some from Malta.'
Sabrina looks worried. 'Do you think anyone will remember?' she asks.
Fiona hopes so. There is nothing in the world like *qubbajt*.

Sabrina stops in front of a clothes shop. 'Isn't that a pretty dress?' Fiona says. Sabrina agrees. But she has already chosen her new dress for Great Siege Day. Mum took her all the way to Oxford Street in London to buy it.

'Maybe Mum will buy me that one,' Fiona says. 'Dad says that we must all wear new clothes for a *festa*. A very long time ago the Maltese couldn't afford to buy new clothes. But they always wore their best on a *festa*. It showed their Patron Saint how much they loved him.

This year the 8th of September happens to be a Sunday. Fiona wakes up early. 'Is it time for breafast?' she asks. Sabrina gives her a glass of water. 'You can't eat breakfast before Holy Communion,' she warns. 'You must be *sajam*.'

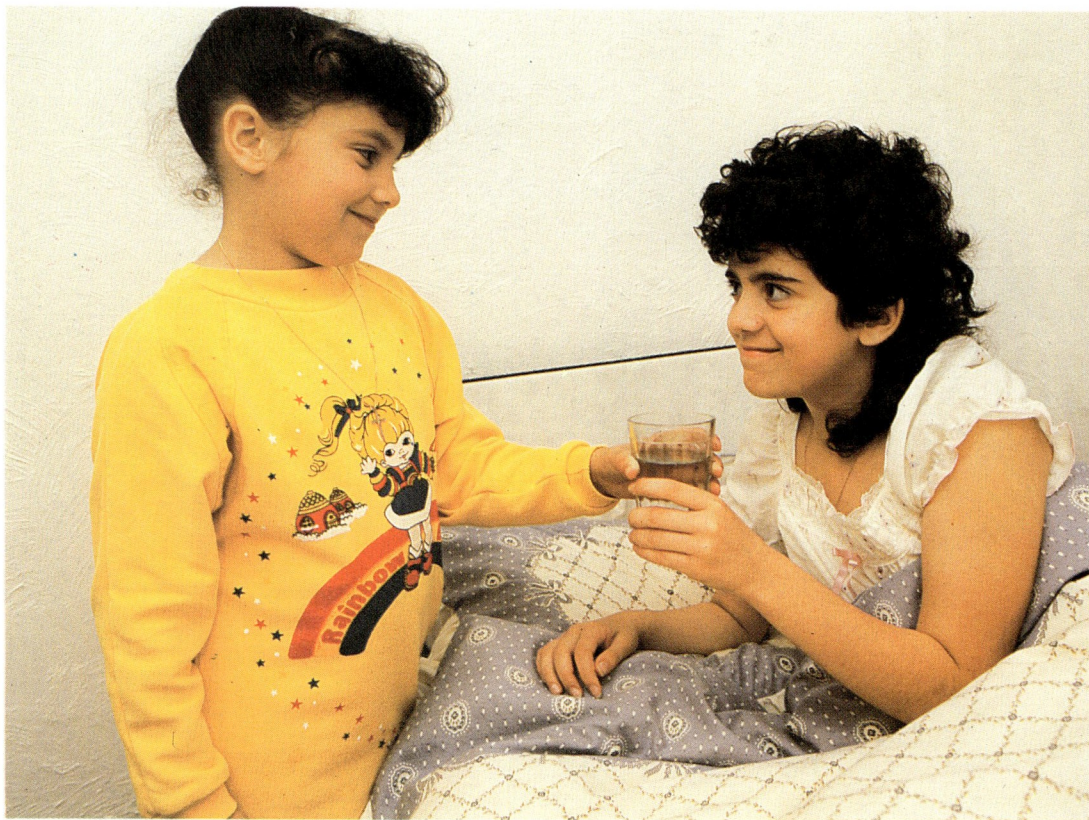

Fiona groans. 'It's very difficult to remember not to eat when you are surrounded by good food.' But she knows it's very important to fast before communion.

A wonderful smell of cooking fills the house. Mum is cooking a special meal. There is rabbit stewing in the pot.

The church is next to Fiona's school.
Inside people are listening to some hymns. The priest starts the
Mass. He is not Maltese but he knows what day it is.

His sermon is all about the Blessed Virgin's love for mankind. Fiona
feels very proud to be one of Her followers.

When the altar boy rings a bell Fiona steps up to the altar to receive Holy Communion. Sabrina is too young to take the Holy Wafer. She has to stay behind in her seat.

'When I'm seven,' she thinks, 'I'll be able to take the Wafer too.' A lot of people receive Holy Communion. Many of them are Maltese. Sabrina recognises her friend Martin. Martin smiles.

After Mass everyone walks home. 'I'm starving,' Fiona says.
Mum checks the cooking. Nothing is burned or overcooked.
Ding-dong. 'That's the doorbell,' Mum says. 'It must be the
Stivalas.'

All the family goes outside to welcome their friends home. Everyone shakes hands and says *merhba*. This is the Maltese word for welcome. Everyone is welcome in a Maltese home on Great Siege Day.

'I have a present for you,' Martin says. He opens a bag. Everyone takes a Perlina.
'Mine is blue,' Fiona says. Sabrina's is pink. 'Can I change it for a white one?' she asks Martin.

Dad feels hungry. 'Let's eat,' he says. Mum invites everyone to sit around the table. She and Dad sit at both ends. The children sit on one side and Mr and Mrs Stivala on the other. Mum puts the food on the table.

'I'm starving,' complains Fiona for the tenth time. She cannot stop her tummy making funny noises as Mum places the stewed rabbit on the table.
'Careful,' Martin says. 'Don't spill sauce on the tablecloth.'

Mum spoons rabbit stew on everyone's spaghetti. Dad tells everyone to stand up and make the sign of the cross. He recites a small prayer, thanking the Blessed Virgin for giving the Maltese enough to eat.

Mum has cooked so much rabbit that no one can possibly eat it all, not even Sabrina.

'I'm full up,' Mrs Stivala says.

Dad smiles. 'There's still dessert left.'

Sabrina can't make up her mind what to have for afters. 'Shall I have the *halva* or the *kannolli*?' she asks.

The *halva* is a Mediterranean sweet which Mum buys from a special shop down the road.

The *kannolli* are delicious pastry tubes stuffed with angelica and sweetened ricotta. Mum and Mrs Stivala made them at home.

After dinner Mrs Stivala helps Mum clean up.

Out in the garden it's very warm. Everyone sits in the sun and listens to Dad telling stories about Malta. Most of them are pirate tales and some are quite frightening.
Everyone eats peanuts and olives to stop them from getting scared.

'Time for bed,' Dad calls to Fiona and Sabrina. The girls change into their nighties.
Ouch – there's something hard under Fiona's pillow.

It's a parcel with Maltese stamps on it. The address is written in Gran's handwriting.
Sabrina wants to open the parcel herself. 'Careful,' Fiona says. 'The present inside must be fragile.'

Sabrina tears off the wrapping. She finds two slabs of *qubbajt*. One is brown and one is white.

'Can we taste it now?' she asks. Fiona is too full up to eat anything else. 'Let's share them with the others at school.'

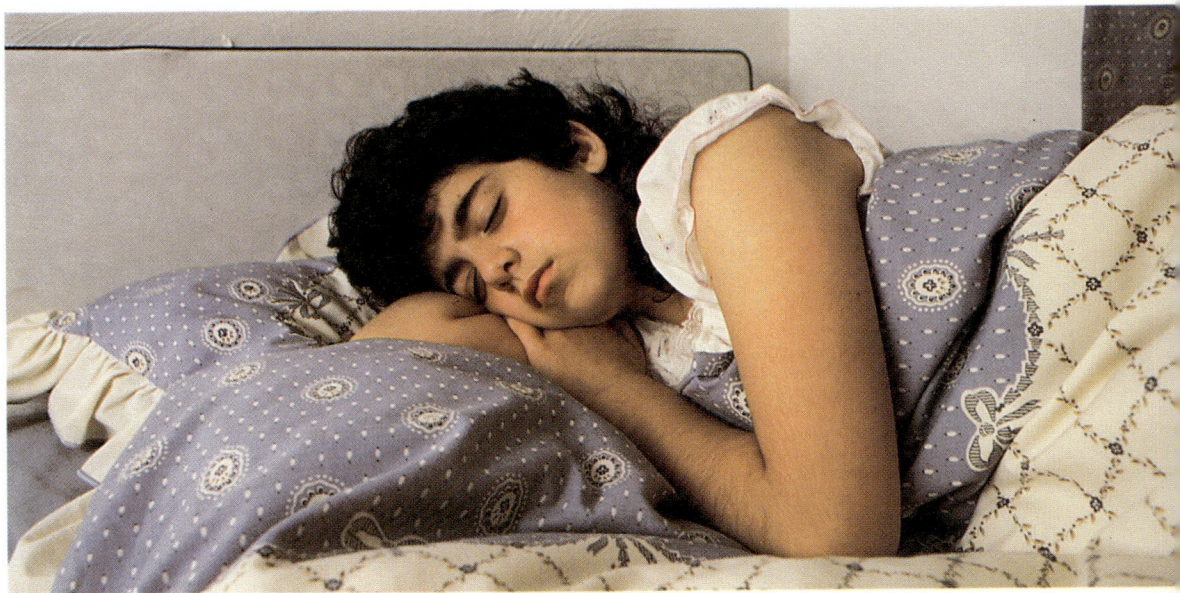

Fiona agrees. The children at school have never tasted *qubbajt*.

LINKED